Sarah Elizabeth Dawes

Light from the Star of Bethlehem

A Poem

Sarah Elizabeth Dawes

Light from the Star of Bethlehem
A Poem

ISBN/EAN: 9783337409005

Printed in Europe, USA, Canada, Australia, Japan

Cover: Foto ©Andreas Hilbeck / pixelio.de

More available books at **www.hansebooks.com**

LIGHT

FROM THE

STAR OF BETHLEHEM.

A POEM.

BY

Mrs. S. E. DAWES,

Author of "Lindenwood," "Hours with Mamma." &c.

"There shall come a star out of Jacob, and a sceptre shall rise out of Israel."

"Behold, there came wise men from the east to Jerusalem, saying, We have seen his star in the east, and have come to worship him."

"And lo! the star which they saw in the east went before them. till it came and stood over where the young child was."

"I am the root and the offspring of David, and the bright and morning star."

L I G H T

FROM

THE STAR OF BETHLEHEM.

Ye seraphs! strike your harps of gold,
The wondrous love of God unfold;
Bid all the angelic host arise,
And with their anthems rend the skies.
A nobler theme than angel tongue
Through heaven's high arches ever sung
Now bids you raise your loftiest strain,
To praise the Babe on Bethlehem's plain.
Hark! how the heavenly chorus breaks,
Each angel voice with joy awakes!

Through highest heaven the anthem rings,
Jesus descends, the King of kings!
All glory be to God on high,
Let earth give back the loud reply,
And join to hail the Saviour's birth,
Who brings good-will and peace on earth.
See! yonder shines his glorious star
That guides the wise men from afar,
Who come with gifts and spices sweet
To offer at the Infant's feet.
Ye shepherds, haste, with one accord,
To greet your Saviour and your Lord.
Fear not though angel voices speak,
And bid you now the manger seek,
Where, in a lowly stable stall,
Lies the Almighty Lord of all!
Let earth to all her thousands tell,
Incarnate God with man doth dwell,
Their woes to heal, their sins to cure,
And make them holy, just, and pure.

Ye mortals, trace his bright career,

While, doing good, he wandered here.

Behold him when a gentle child,

Sporting among the mountains wild,

Or roaming o'er the valleys green,

Wearing always a thoughtful mien;

And when the tribes of Israel haste

From palmy plain and desert waste,

To keep each year the law divine

That called them to their nation's shrine,

He enters with his parents there,

To mingle in the nation's prayer.

But, toiling up the mountain height,

Their anxious faces pale with fright.

Retracing step by step the way,

Two weary parents sadly stray.

Their son, the meek and holy child,

Who cheered them late with accents mild,

They seek in vain o'er vale and hill,

While fearful thoughts their bosoms fill.

2

Among their kindred he is not,
And vain they search each favorite spot.
Then back to Zion's summit high
They turn with hope their anxious eye,
And there, within the temple's wall,
The wonder and the gaze of all,
Among the wise of Israel's land
The fearless child doth calmly stand.
With meekness beams his sweet young
    face,
Yet still he speaks with manly grace.
A wondrous light around him plays,
That forms a halo with its rays;
And o'er that brow, so full of grace,
A beauty not of earth they trace.
Amazed the sages gaze around,
And listen all with awe profound.
"Can this the child of Mary be,
The son of Joseph, that we see?"
And while they thus these thoughts re-
    volve,

And strive in vain the doubt to solve,
Within their midst these parents stand,
With awe-struck look and trembling hand.
The scene that to their eye reveals,
Their bloodless lips with wonder seals.
The mother then, with chiding tone,
That spake her love and care alone,
Addressed him thus, her truant child,
Whom she had sought with anguish wild:
"My son, how wrongly thou hast dealt
With us who pangs of sorrow felt!
Say wherefore didst thou linger here,
Thy parents' hearts to rend with fear.
Thy father and I amid the throng,
In search of thee have wandered long.
Among thy kindred we have sought,
But they of thee could tell us nought.
Thy cheerful zeal and ready will
Our slightest wish to e'er fulfil,
Hath made us fear some dreadful blow

Had made, perchance, thy life-blood flow;
And with their loved one thus to part
Hath sorely tried thy parents' heart."
Then with his gaze uplifted high,
With reverent look and moistened eye,
Young Jesus spake, in calmest mood,
To those who thus reproving stood:
"Why, wist ye not 'twas time thy son
His Father's work on earth begun?"
He ceased; and all with silent awe,
With reverence from his side withdraw,
And each to others look in vain, —
His doubtful words could none explain.
His brow was stamped with high command
As now he stood with lifted hand;
His mind seemed raised, in one short hour,
From childhood's state to manhood's power.
Then gliding down the lofty height
Whither his spirit had taken flight,
He girt his childish robes around,

And with his parents then was found,
With them to seek his humble home,
And from their side no more to roam,
Until in manhood he should stand,
Ordained a priest in Judah's land.
Obedient to each wish expressed,
His parents' hearts he ever blessed;
And while he thus in favor grew,
He gained in wisdom and stature too.
His mother oft in deepest thought,
To solve his words all vainly sought;
And when he spake in accents blest,
Hid deep within her yearning breast
She placed each word, and pondered o'er
The mystic meaning that they bore.

Thus swiftly passed his youthful time,
Till grown at length to manhood's prime;
And then, by prophets long foretold,
There came Elias the preacher bold,

And crying, "Now prepare the way
To own Messiah's rightful sway.
Hill, vale, and mount shall levelled be,
And all shall his salvation see."
Clad in a robe of camel's hair,
He fed on wild and simple fare,
And led a guileless, holy life,
Removed from care and worldly strife.
The people came from far and near,
And thronged in crowds his words to hear.
His language free, impassioned, bold,
He cries, "I'm not the Christ foretold:
He cometh soon with mightier hand,
And power that I may not command.
I bow to him with reverence due,
Unworthy even to loose his shoe."
And while he speaks each burning word,
A strange but gentle step is heard.
The prophet turns with anxious eye,
And seeth Jesus passing by.

He pauses near the river side,
Where Jordan's waters swiftly glide;
And thus addressing the preacher, cries,
"I come that thou may'st me baptize."
Amazed at this his strange request,
'Put forth with power and high behest,
Forbidding looks came o'er his face,
And thus he spake with humble grace:
"There's need that I should pardoned be,
And washed from all my sins by thee.
Comest thou to a worm of earth,
When thou dost boast celestial birth?
"Suffer," said Jesus, "this sacred rite,
That I may thus the law requite."

But lo! what means the glory now
That hovers o'er his radiant brow?
Sweet visions greet his raptured sight,
And round him pour a flood of light.
The eternal Spirit like a dove

Descends on him from realms above;
And with a voice of sweetest sound
Proclaims the blissful tidings round:
This is my own beloved Son,
Behold the high and lofty one!

This done, he left the wondering throng,
Led by the Spirit's power along,
And came to where a desert wild
Had ne'er with flowers or verdure smiled,
But all was barren waste and drear,
A scene devoid of earthly cheer;
There slowly passed each weary day,
And lingering wore the night away;
For he who owned earth's varied store
Was fainting there with hunger sore.
Then cometh he the tempter vile
Whose subtle arts did Eve beguile;
And now, with all the deadly hate
That made his heart with foulness great,

He stood before the guileless one,

And thus his vile discourse begun:

"If thou dost boast the high degree

The incarnate Son of God to be,

Then let thy power divinely aid,

And of these stones let bread be made."

But Jesus said, "Hast thou not heard

This truth from out the sacred word:

By bread alone man shall not live,

But God's own mouth his food doth give?"

Again, upon the temple's height

The vile one speaks with tempting might:

"Cast down thyself from hence," he cries:

"'T is written that from yonder skies

An angel host shall be thy stay,

And guard with care thy falling way."

But Jesus saith, "The sacred word

Forbids thee now to tempt the Lord."

Though baffled thus, foul Satan tries

To charm with power the Saviour's eyes;

3

And, touched as if by magic wand,
Far stretching out on either hand
Was spread a scene of glorious view,
Of empires vast and kingdoms new,
With crowns and gems of priceless worth,
And all the hoarded wealth of earth.
The tempter views the bright array
That now lies spread beneath his sway,
And though it wrings his fiendish heart
With all this power and wealth to part,
Yet now he gladly offers all,
That he may cause the Saviour's fall.
He cries, "These things I give to thee
If thou wilt kneel and worship me;
For see, the wealth of earth is mine;
But worship me, and all is thine."
The Saviour calmly placed his eye
On him who stood with malice by;
And, standing forth with noble form,
Addressed him thus in language warm:

"Get far from hence, thou prince of sin!
My worship thou canst never win;
This glittering pomp, this worldly show,
The Son of Man may never know.
Depart from hence! the Lord I serve, —
Tempt me not from his law to swerve!"

And must the son of darkness now
Again before high heaven bow?
Since hurled from off his starry throne,
Where once he sat and proudly shone,
Fierce hate had filled his darkened mind,
And dire revenge he sought to find.
And now behold this tempting hour,
The Son of God was in his power!
His earthly pomp, his treasures vast,
Had been before the Saviour cast;
Yet still unbending, firm, and brave,
Like rocks that breast the foaming wave,
Or like some high and massive tower

That baffles all invading power,
He stood as pure and fair withal
As man once stood before the fall.
Quailing beneath that eye of fire,
The tempter leaves with sullen ire';
And shorn of all his boasting might,
He seeks again the realms of night.

And now o'er all the heavenly plains
Are floating sweet angelic strains;
Triumphant joy in heaven is known,
And bright-winged seraphs round the throne
To earth now wend their shining way,
And to their Maker homage pay.
O earth! prolong the hymns of joy,
And all your highest notes employ.
For he who all your sorrows bore,
And felt this fierce temptation sore,
Can shield and succor every heart
When Satan hurls the tempting dart.

Then Jesus went his toilsome way,
Deep wrongs to suffer day by day;
Yet meekly bearing scorn and shame,
And shunning the path to worldly fame,
The poor in life he chose to be
Attendants on his ministry;
And oft with joy they gathered round
To hear the gospel's joyful sound;
And many besides those favored few
Embraced him as their Saviour true.
His fame went out through all the land,
And sick were brought from every hand.
They came oppressed with divers pains,
And some were held in Satan's chains;
While others madly thronged his way,
Whose minds were lost to reason's sway.
The deaf, the lame, the halt and blind,
All came to him relief to find;
And oft the hymn of joy uprose
From those who felt no more their woes.

In mighty throngs, from far and near
They came, his words of peace to hear;
And hark! methinks from yonder mount
There flow sweet words from wisdom's
    fount.
The Saviour speaks in words of love .
That lift all hearts to heaven above:
"Lo! they are blest in spirit poor,
For their reward is ever sure;
To them shall be this portion given,
To dwell among the joys of heaven.
And blest are they who've sorrow borne,
And here on earth in sadness mourn;
For they shall find me always near,
And I their drooping hearts will cheer.
The meek are blest, for they by birth
Shall evermore possess the earth.
And blest are they who seek to find
The food that fills the hungry mind:
Their souls shall be with blessings fed,

And they shall eat of heavenly bread.

And they are blest whose feeling heart

The gift of mercy doth impart;

For o'er their souls again doth flow

The tide of mercy they bestow.

Again, are blest the pure in heart,

For theirs shall be the glorious part

To see the face of God above,

In yonder world of joy and love.

And blest are they who peaceful make

The path of strife that others take;

For they shall heavenly bliss obtain,

And in my kingdom ever reign.

And blest are ye when men revile

And call you oft the sons of guile:

Let now my words your hearts elate,

For your reward in heaven is great.

Behold, the salt of earth are ye:

Let wide diffused your savor be.

Ye are to earth a shining light:

Your lamps keep ever burning bright.
Ye know a city placed on high
Becomes the observed of every eye;
Then let your light so shine on earth
That all may see and know your worth,
And thus be led to glorify
Your heavenly Father throned on high.
Think not I come to e'er withdraw
One line from Sinai's righteous law:
I come its precepts to instil,
And all its mandates to fulfil;
For verily now I say to you,
That ye shall find my words are true:
Till heaven and earth shall pass away,
The law shall hold its rightful sway;
And every word that God hath willed,
Shall be in all its points fulfilled;
And he who shall rebellious stand,
Or seek to break one least command,
And dare to others teach the same,

Shall be in heaven the least in name.

But he who doth my words obey,

And others lead in righteous way,

Shall in my kingdom dwell in state,

And numbered be among the great.

Again, hath been this saying told

By those who spake in days of old:

Thou shalt to falsehood never bow,

But to the Lord perform thy vow;

But I say now, swear not at all,

Nor on Jehovah lightly call.

Swear not by heaven, for 't is the throne

Where sits the high and holy One;

And by his footstool where we tread

Let not the oath profane be said;

Nor by the holy city swear,

For 't is the Lord's peculiar care.

And heed the words that now I say, —

Let e'er your speech be Yea and Nay;

For whatsoe'er is more than these

4

The prince of evil well doth please.
And ye have heard this saying too:
Repay the evil done to you;
But I a milder precept make, —
Ye shall not angry vengeance take.
Give e'er to him that asketh thee,
And ne'er from want or sorrow flee;
And he who would thy favor gain,
Let not his plea be urged in vain.
It hath been said, Thy neighbor love,
And from a foe thy heart remove;
But I say, love e'en those that hate
And try to make your sorrows great.
Bless them that curse, and pray for those
Who heap upon you bitter woes,
That ye may all the children be
Of Him who rules in equity,
And causeth e'er the sun to rise
The same on all below the skies,
And sendeth rain and nightly dew

Alike on just and unjust too.

Take heed your alms ye do not give

That ye may have a name to live;

Nor do not sound a trumpet loud

To gain the homage of the crowd;

And never let thy left hand know

The gift thy right hand doth bestow;

For while thine alms in secret be,

The Lord, who doth thy motives see,

Shall thee reward with open hand,

And thou shalt in his favor stand.

And when thou prayest, do not use

Vain words that God will e'er refuse;

For He who hears the faintest sigh

Will not regard a mocking cry,

Nor bend to earth a willing ear

The pompous words of pride to hear.

But when thou prayest, thou shalt go

Where none but God thy words can know;

And when within thy closet there

Lift up to him thy secret prayer;
And from thy Father have reward,
For he doth hear each secret word,
And knoweth e'er the things ye need,
And all your wants doth kindly heed;
But bids you ask his daily care,
And this shall be your form of prayer:

"Our Father who art in heaven now,
Before thy throne we humbly bow.
All hallowed be thy sacred name;
Oh, let us now thy blessing claim.
Thy kingdom come; and may thy reign
Extended be o'er earth's domain.
Thy will be done as 't is in heaven,
And praises due be ever given.
Give us this day our daily bread, —
'T is from thy hand we all are fed.
Forgive in heaven the debt we owe,
As we should e'er forgive below;

And lead us not, in fatal hour,
To fall before the tempter's power,
But from all evil keep us free;
And thine the power and glory be,
And thine the kingly right to reign
For evermore on earth: Amen.

"If ye to men forgive their sin,
Ye shall your Father's pardon win;
For he your sins will not forgive
If unforgiving ye shall live.
And when ye fast, be not like those
Who mar their face by unfelt woes,
And sadness o'er their visage cast,
That they to men may seem to fast;
For verily now to you I say,
Their God this sin will sure repay.
But when thou fastest, o'er thy head
Let fragrant ointment sweet be shed;
And wash thy face, that thou appear

Not unto men to fast in fear,
But to thy Father, who doth see
The secret thoughts that dwell with thee;
And thy reward he shall bestow,
That all thy secret worth may know.
Lay not upon this fleeting earth
Your treasures all of sordid worth,
Where moth and rust and early blight
Remove them from thy eager sight,
And thieves break through and steal away
Thy hoarded stores and rich array.
There is a world where grief and woe
The dwellers there can never know,
And moth and rust no more will creep
Where God doth heavenly treasures keep.
In that bright realm lay up your store,
And thus be blest for evermore;
For where your treasure hath a part,
E'en there will also be your heart.
Again, I say ye shall not take

Anxious thought for the body's sake,
Nor eager ask, What shall we eat?
Is not your life worth more than meat?
Behold the fowls that cleave the air
With pinions light and plumage fair;
Unknown to care, with joy they sing,
Or upward mount with rapid wing;
They do not sow nor ever reap,
Yet God doth all in kindness keep.
And are ye not of better mould,
The heirs of heaven and joys untold?
And which of you, by taking thought,
Can add unto his stature aught?
And why do ye with thoughtful mind
Your outward raiment seek to find?
Behold the lilies how they grow:
No weary toil they ever know;
In robes of snow all purely white
They stud the fields like gems of light;
They do not spin from day to day,

Yet unto you this truth I say,
That Israel's king in wisdom great,
Adorned in glorious robes of state,
And seated on his regal throne,
Was by this floweret far outshone.
If God so clothe the grassy field
That doth its verdant harvest yield
That only blooms but for a day,
And then is thrown like chaff away,
Say, will he not more ready be
Your every want to kindly see?
And will he not your clothing give,
O ye of little faith to live?
Then do not of these trifles think,
Nor anxious ask, What shall we drink,
And where shall daily food be had,
And wherewithal shall we be clad?
The Gentiles seek with anxious mind,
And strive these worldly things to find;
But God who dwells in heaven above

Regards you e'er with eyes of love,
And knoweth all your earthly need,
And hears whene'er you humbly plead.
Then seek ye first the narrow way,
And let your footsteps never stray;
And while from every sin ye flee,
Behold, these things shall added be.
Ye shall not look with troubled eyes
To see the morrow's sun arise :
Each coming day will bring its share
Of earthly joy and earthly care;
And ever will the day suffice
For all the evils that arise.

"Judge not; for, as your judgment be,
Thus shall it be returned to thee.
And e'en I say, your measures too
Shall measured be again to you.
And why beholdest thou the mote
That through thy brother's eye doth float,

5

And seest not the larger beam
That now within thine eye doth gleam?
First cast the beam that dwells in thee,
And make thyself from error free;
And then more clear shalt thou espy
The mote within thy brother's eye.
Again, I say, — my words believe, —
Whate'er ye ask ye shall receive;
And while ye seek with willing mind,
Your souls shall heavenly blessings find.
And when at mercy's gates ye knock,
Its doors to you shall e'er unlock.
What man is there whose son did plead
For bread to help in time of need,
Would ever act the wicked part,
And give a stone, with hardened heart?
If, then, a father's love is shown
To ye who are to evil prone,
Then how much more shall God above
Behold you with a father's love!

Then whatsoe'er ye would that men
Should do to you, do so to them;
For this hath been by prophets told,
And read within your laws of old.
Consider well your future state,
And enter in at mercy's gate;
In paths of folly never stray,
For wide the gate, and broad the way,
That leadeth on to sin and woe,
And many through its portals go;
But strait and narrow is the way
That leadeth on to realms of day,
And few there be, with pardoned sin,
That find the way, and walk therein.
Beware of prophets false and fair,
Who clothing soft of goodness wear:
Without, they seem devoid of sin,
Yet they are ravening wolves within;
For by their fruits ye e'er can know
The good and evil here below;

For do ye gather from the thorn
The grape that doth the vine adorn?
Or does the thistle ever bear
The fruit that crowns the fig-tree fair?
'T is even so, good fruit shall be
For ever found on thrifty tree;
And evil trees shall e'er bring forth
Their fruit corrupt and void of worth.
Not every one that saith to me,
Lord, Lord, shall e'er my kingdom see:
But he a throne of joy shall fill
Who doeth e'er my Father's will.
When fearful dawns the last great day,
Lord, Lord, shall many eager say;
We have professed thy holy name,
And wonders wrought e'en by the same;
Then I will say, I know you not;
Upon you rests a sinful blot;
Far from my face ye shall depart
Who sin have wrought with evil heart.

Then whosoe'er these sayings hear,
And doeth them with holy fear,
Shall be like him with wisdom filled,
Who on a rock his house did build.
The winds of heaven blew around,
And rain descended o'er the ground;
The torrents roared with fearful might;
But far upon that rocky height,
Unharmed by all the swelling flood,
This wise man's dwelling firmly stood,
Nor felt the tempest's fearful shock, —
'T was founded on the solid rock.
But he that doeth not my word,
Although my sayings he hath heard,
Lo! I will liken him to one
Who built his house the sand upon.
And when the wind with fury roared,
And swift the rushing torrent poured,
The house thus built upon the sand
The raging storm could not withstand.

It fell; and, spreading far around,
The broken fragments strewed the ground."

The waves were bounding blithe and free
Upon Judea's restless sea,
And balmy breezes gently bore
A noble ship from off the shore.
She carried freight of richer worth
Than all the treasures vast of earth.
In calm repose the Saviour slept
While watchful eyes their vigils kept.
They gaze around the tranquil sky,
And soon dark clouds come floating by;
They deepen, darken, spread around,
Till soon is heard the tempest's sound;
On, on they come, with fearful might,
Like warriors armed for deadly fight.
The lightnings flash and blaze afar,
And fearful rolls the thunder-car.
The heaving billows mount on high,

And seem to meet the angry sky.
The hoarse wind now with fury raves,
And higher mount the raging waves.
But yet, mid all this fearful scene,
The Saviour's sleep is still serene.
His faithful followers, pale with fear,
Now fly to him for words of cheer.
"Awake! arise!" they trembling cry;
"Oh, save us, Lord, or else we die!"
Unmoved, he saith, "What means your
    fear?
For know ye not your Lord is here?
O ye of little faith! now see
That e'en the tempest bows to me:
Ye winds and waves, obey my will;
Your God commands you: Peace, be still!"
That voice above the stormy roar
Was heard with fear from shore to shore;
And over all the troubled deep
There came a calm unbroken sleep;

All nature heard the high behest,
And sank in stillness deep to rest.

The Saviour oft, at close of day,
Far from the city haunts away,
To Bethany's peaceful, happy home
With weary feet would gladly roam.
There, listening to his converse sweet,
Sat Mary at her Master's feet;
While Martha thought her office blest
To serve with care their noble guest.
But Mary chose the wiser part,
To store with truth her youthful heart,
And honored thought her humble seat,
Low at her blessed Saviour's feet;
While Martha, cumbered with worldly care,
But seldom joined her sister there,
And much preferred with viands rare
To sweeten her Master's simple fare.
Their brother, too, was often heard

To urge his stay with welcome word;
And thus within this loved retreat,
With pious friends would Jesus meet.
Within that home, in fatal hour,
Came Death in all his dreaded power.
The mournful news to Jesus flies,
Lazarus now in Bethany dies;
And, sad at heart, his footsteps stray
Within the well-remembered way.
But, ere he reached the scene of woe,
The tide of life had ceased to flow.
The weeping sisters round him came,
Most sadly calling on his name,
And saying, "Master, our brother dear
Would not have died hadst thou been
      here."
And Jesus seeing their anguish deep,
And those around so sadly weep,
He bade them hope, though deep the gloom
That gathered round their brother's tomb.

6

But when he heard the weeping crowd,
Who mourned the dead with voices loud,
And saw within that dreary place
The form he loved, in death's embrace,
The weight of grief his heart had kept,
Burst wildly forth; and Jesus wept.
Then, drying his tears, with mighty power
Becoming that triumphant hour,
He raised above his beaming eye,
And prayed to Him who dwells on high:
"I thank thee, Father, thou hast heard,
And given me power to speak the word.
This unbelieving throng shall see
That I am equal now with thee."
Then, stretching forth his Godlike hand,
He raised his voice in high command.
"Behold my power, ye men of earth:
Lazarus, I bid thee now come forth!"
Death heard the strange, all-powerful tone,
And trembled on his rocking throne.

The Son of God had burst his chain,
The dead returned to life again!
Erect he stood, a living form,
With quickened pulse and vigor warm,
And, loosing vestments of the tomb,
Appeared again in healthful bloom.
The soul encased in mortal frame,
Lit up with holier light the same;
While, changing oft, the speaking eye
Proclaimed anew life's victory.

Then sealed were lips that late reviled,
And paled were faces that once had smiled,
When Jesus oft, with mighty power,
Had made e'en Satan's hosts to cower.
And some, with hate and frenzied rage,
Against his cause with zeal engage;
And from that time, with fell intent
They sought where'er the Saviour went.
No more among the city's throng

Could he in safety tarry long;
But, far amid some wild retreat,
His faithful few he oft would meet.
There, neath the vaulted dome of heaven,
Were his sublimest precepts given.
There from his lips each glowing line
With beauty fell and power divine.
In vain they sought, with malice deep,
A watch upon his words to keep,
And thus from them to prove his cause
High treason against Cæsar's laws.
While thus pursued and sore oppressed,
One place he found of peaceful rest,
From whence, when filled with care and
    woe,
The tears of grief for him would flow.
To that dear home one eve he sped,
Where Lazarus lived who once was dead;
And there, while sitting with friends around,
A box of ointment Mary found.

She meekly sought her wonted seat,
And bathed with this her Saviour's feet;
And while they dripped with perfume rare,
She wiped them with her flowing hair.
The incense from those blessed feet
Filled all the house with odors sweet;
But envious eyes surveyed the scene,
And Judas spake with subtle mien:
"Why all this waste of ointment rare
That Mary now seems not to spare?
It might have been with profit sold,
And furnished many poor with gold."
'T was not because the poor he loved,
That this sad waste his bosom moved,
But 't was his thievish hand that bore
The bag that held the shining ore.
Jesus turned an approving eye
On her who stood with trembling by;
And sweetly flowed his words of cheer:
"I cannot always tarry here,

While those with whom grim want doth
    hide
Will ever here on earth abide.
Then chide her not: this sweet perfume
Anoints my body for the tomb."

The morrow's sun rose clear and bright
On glorious scenes to mortal sight.
To Salem's gates a mighty throng
Attended Israel's King along.
Beneath his feet were garments spread,
And palm-leaves waved around his head.
But hark! we hear the joyful cries
And clear hosannas pealing rise;
The sounding anthems loudly ring,
With holy zeal his followers sing.
Hosannas now in highest strains
Float through Judea's palmy plains;
While every echoing hillside's voice
In answering chorus sings Rejoice!

"Blessed is he that cometh now,
Before his kingly presence bow;
The Lord hath sent him in his name,
The joyful tidings wide proclaim."
They reach the temple's open gate,
While eager crowds around them wait.
He enters there; but o'er his face
A shade of sorrow steals apace.
Beneath the temple's lofty dome
Vain merchandise had found a home;
While those who cared for nought but gold,
Within its walls both bought and sold,
And sinful crowds were treading there
Within his Father's house of prayer.
But list! what sound breaks on his ear,
And lights his face with kindly cheer?
An infant band his name adore,
And loud their joyful anthems pour.
The temple with their chorus rings,
Hosanna to the King of kings!

The Saviour comes! and babes now raise
Their infant voices in his praise.
While louder yet ascends their song,
With wonder stand the listening throng.
They ask of Christ, in scornful way,
"Dost hear what these young children say?"
"Yea," answered he, with beaming eye:
"Dost hear not in their joyful cry
The words that from a prophet's tongue
Within your laws for years have rung, —
'From babes God hath perfected praise,
And sucklings too their voices raise'?"

The Passover now was near at hand,
And Jesus issued this command:
"Go forth within the city gate;
An open door for thee shall wait,
And thou shalt enter a mansion there,
And straight an upper room prepare."
With willing feet his followers sped,

And found it e'en as Christ had said.
And when all things were fitly placed,
The Master then the table graced;
And while he sat, a halo bright
His placid brow encrowned with light.
With saddened face the bread he brake,
And thus unto the twelve he spake:
"As now ye eat, remember too
My broken body slain for you;
And as ye take the wine-cup red,
Behold the blood that I have shed.
I leave you soon; but still my hand
Shall comfort oft this little band.
My hour of darkness now draws near;
A traitor lurks, yea, even here."
All gaze around with anxious eye,
And trembling ask, "Lord, is it I?"
But Jesus mildly saith, "'T is he
Who eateth now the bread with me."
And reaching forth his hand divine,

7

He gave to Judas the fatal sign.
Then straightway Satan entered in,
And filled his heart with deadly sin.
No more could he with subtle face,
With pious looks that table grace;
But forth he went, while malice vile
Raged fierce within that son of guile.
The powers of darkness held his heart,
And bade him act the traitor's part.

But lo! on Olive's midnight brow
Another scene is passing now.
Low kneeling in a garden there,
A sacred head is bowed in prayer.
He feels upon his shoulders hurled
The weight of all a sinful world.
Alone he prays, that sainted form,
Through all that night of mental storm.
Such burdened thoughts his bosom fill,
That drops of blood like rain distil.

"Father, remove this cup from me,
If now it seemeth good to thee;
In mercy hear thy bleeding Son;
But yet thy will, not mine, be done."
And as the suppliant turns his eye,
A shining one is standing by.
Down from the heavenly courts above
To earth he comes on wings of love;
And now within that waiting ear
He whispers words of holy cheer.
Then back he wings his upward flight
Among the shining sons of light.
Jesus receives the heavenly balm,
And riseth now with bosom calm.
His time is near; yet o'er his face
No shade of sorrow finds a place.
He feels new strength; and, nerved with
   power,
He waits the dark betraying hour.

And from a covert close at hand
There issue forth a murderous band;
And Judas leads their ranks along,
More vile than all the fiendish throng;
And stepping forth with stealthy pace,
He kisses now his Master's face;
And, lest this base design should fail,
With mocking voice he bids him "Hail!"
Receiving thus the traitor's sign,
They seize upon that form divine,
And, eager for their captive's fall,
They lead to Pilate's judgment-hall;
There, ranged around on either hand,
Are placed the false accusing band;
While meekly he who knew no guile,
Before them stands in durance vile.
But now upon that ruler's face
Both fear and pity find a place.
His captive free from sin doth seem.
He thinks upon the warning dream,

And fain would heed his pleading wife,
And save in peace that just One's life.
But louder sounds the fearful cry,
"This base impostor crucify!
Let this his guilty portion be, —
Away, away, to Calvary!"
Such angry faces round him lower,
He trembles for his seat of power;
And straight the awful charge is given,
To crucify the Lord of heaven!
With fiendish joy they seize him now,
And crown with thorns that noble brow;
And, robed in purple, Jesus stands,
And feels the scourge of Jewish hands.
Within his hand a reed they place,
And bend the knee with mocking grace;
And while such deeds the crowd amuse,
They hail him "King of all the Jews."
But Jesus speaks no murmuring word,
And from his lips no sigh is heard,

While they with such malignant hate
Deride and mock his kingly state.
He meekly bears their cruel blows,
While o'er his form the life-blood flows.
Pilate surveys the fiendish scene
With troubled eye and thoughtful mien.
"His blood," he cries, "I will not bear;
Ye know his life I fain would spare.
No stain shall on my garments stay,
Behold, I wash my guilt away."
Then all the Jews, with fearful cry,
Pronounce their doom with voices high:
"On us and on our children be
The blood that flows from Calvary!
His crimes deserve the avenging rod, —
He claims the name of Son of God!
Our laws decree that he must die, —
This boasting King we 'll crucify!"
With shouts of triumph, one and all
They march without the judgment-hall;

While Jesus follows with feeble frame,
And bears along his cross of shame.
He calmly meets his cruel fate,
Yet sinks beneath the crushing weight;
And thus compelled to lend his aid,
The cross is soon on Simon laid.
They onward march, that bloody throng,
Through verdant hills and vales along;
While far behind, with cries of woe,
The feeble women follow slow.
A sadder scene beneath the sky
Was ne'er revealed to mortal eye.
The great Messiah, of heavenly birth,
To death was borne by worms of earth!

And now beneath Golgotha's sky
They place the cross uplifted high,
And on it nail their Saviour now,
While high above his regal brow
They place the name their hearts refuse,

"Jesus of Nazareth, King of Jews."
A thief was placed on either side,
And both with him were crucified;
And thus was Jesus doomed to be
With sinners nailed to the accursed tree.
Mingled wine and myrrh they take,
And offer this, his thirst to slake;
While, often pierced, his bleeding side
Poured forth to earth a crimson tide.
No hand could heal that flowing wound,
Though weeping friends stood all around.
His hour had come, his time of woe,
And earth and heaven felt the blow.
With taunting words they pass him by,
And lift their mocking voices high:
"If thou canst save thyself, descend;
Before thy power we then will bend."
But Jesus answers not a word, —
This prayer for them alone is heard:
"Father, they know not what they do;

In mercy hear, and pardon too."
Fierce tortures rack his human frame,
And thus he calls on Heaven's name:
"O my God, say why hast thou
Thy dying Son forsaken now!"
But hark! there comes a fearful sound,
And earth's foundations heave around.
Huge rocks are rent on either hand,
While darkness broods o'er all the land.
The sun in grief withholds his light,
And veils the earth in darkest night.
Convulsed, all nature feels the shock,
And hills with fear and trembling rock.
They seem to feel his mighty throes,
And mourn their great Creator's woes.
"My God! my God!" again he cries,
And lo! the Lord of Glory dies!
Forth starting at the fearful sound,
The dead arise and stand around.
The temple's veil is rent in twain,
8

And fearful heaves the earth again.
They saw with fear the darkened sun,
And all the things that there were done;
And those who stood with trembling by,
With pallid lips were forced to cry,
"'T is true! the Son of God is he
Who now is nailed to yonder tree!"
In haste the gloomy scene they leave,
While many hearts with fear believe.
When 'all but they the cross had fled,
Three women lingered round the dead;
Deep anguish rent their bleeding heart,
From their dear Lord they soon must part.
Though last of all, they tarried yet,
Till veiled in gloom the sun had set.
When evening shades had gathered round,
At Pilate's house was Joseph found,
And craved the noble form of him
Who lay mid Calvary's shadows dim.
And Pilate, who feared some mystic power,

Gave them their boon the selfsame hour.
And now they haste, a mournful crowd,
And soon their Saviour's form enshroud;
And there, beneath the midnight gloom,
They lay him in the rocky tomb;
And sealing the door, they then depart,
With streaming eyes and sorrowing heart.

Now when the morning splendors bright
Bathed all the mountain-tops in light,
And through the gorgeous eastern gate
The king of day came forth in state, —
The first glad day of the blessed week, —
The Marys came their Lord to seek,
And stood around his new-made tomb
With weeping eyes and hearts of gloom.
But now they all with sad amaze
Each to the other fearful gaze.
Beneath they hear a mighty sound
That trembling shakes the solid ground.

The hills with fearful echoes ring,
When swift on bright celestial wing,
Down from the blissful realms on high,
An angel form flits through the sky.
Straight to the tomb he wings his way,
And rolls the massive stone away.
The women in that sacred place
Bend low to seek their Master's face;
But found, instead, an angel bright
Was sitting there in robes of white;
And pointing to the linen shroud,
With soothing voice he spake aloud:
"Why this affright? ye need not fear:
Your Lord is risen, he is not here;
And now, behold, the life-blood warm
Is coursing through his living form.
Go, haste, the tidings quickly tell,
That joy in other hearts may dwell.
The news to you I now proclaim, —
With joyful haste go spread the same."

They eager fly with rapid feet,
When soon a stately form they meet ;
And while he speaks, their faces pale, —
With well-known voice he cries, " All
    hail ! "
And thus he calms their every fear :
" 'T is Jesus' voice that now ye hear.
Go quickly and my brethren tell
That with their Saviour all is well."
Then o'er their souls a rushing tide
Of wildest joy again doth glide ;
And kneeling round, with one accord
They bow before their risen Lord.
Again on joyful wings they fly,
With swelling heart and sparkling eye ;
And soon their blissful story spread,
That Christ is risen from the dead !
Surprised they listened to the word,
And doubted much what they had heard.
Like idle tales their tidings seemed,

As though perchance the women dreamed.
But Peter ran with fiery zeal,
Their words of mystery to reveal;
And when he sought amid the gloom,
And found not Jesus in the tomb,
He wondered at the strange event,
And thoughtful on his way he went.

All nature smiled with radiance bright
Beneath the morning's golden light,
And flowers of fairest form and hue
Were glittering with gilded dew,
And stamped upon each verdant sod
Was seen the hand of nature's God;
And moving things with joy seemed rife,
As grateful for the boon of life.
But two sad forms, mid all this scene,
To Emmaus walked, with saddened mien.
Their hearts were filled with bitter woe
As on they went with footsteps slow.

No other theme employed their tongue
Save he who on the cross had hung;
And while they spake, a listening ear
To hear their words to them drew near.
"What things are these ye sadly tell?
On whom have such dire judgments fell?"
"Art thou a stranger here?" they cried,
"And hast not heard how Jesus died?
A mighty One in word and deed,
We trusted he would Israel lead
In arms victorious o'er our foes,
And vengeance take for all our woes,
And on Mount Zion's turrets high
Would lift our banner to the sky,
And, vexed by Roman power no more,
Our ancient realm again restore;
But all our fondest hopes have died, —
The great Messiah they've crucified!
And seeing his form no more below,
Our hearts are filled with deepest woe.

Three days of sorrow now have fled
Since he was numbered with the dead;
And now, behold, another woe
Hath made our tears again to flow:
The form we buried with tender care
Has now been borne we know not where."
With kindling eye the stranger spake:
"Why now do ye this mourning make?"
Then pointing back to days of yore,
He spoke of all a prophet's lore
That told how Christ should die for men,
And on the third day rise again.
And as they near the village drew,
They made the stranger welcome too;
And said, "Abide with us, we pray,
For yonder fades the light of day."
But when he blessed the bread and brake,
And bade them all a portion take,
Their eyes were opened then to see
'T was he who hung on Calvary;

And while they gazed with fond delight,
He vanished from their mortal sight.

'T was morn; and on each mountain height
The sun poured forth his glories bright;
Hill, vale, and wood and dewy plain
As brightly glowed as if no stain
Or blighting curse o'er this fair earth
To human woes had given birth.
The holy city, crowned with light,
Stood forth in all her queenly might;
The temple, with its golden spires,
Seemed glowing with celestial fires;
The massive towers of Zion rose
In proud array 'gainst hostile foes;
The palm-trees waved their graceful arms,
As conscious all of morning charms;
Each tender herb and floweret fair
Sent perfumes sweet through all the air.
The rose of Sharon, fresh with dew,

Breathed forth its fragrant praise anew;
While sweetly bloomed the lily pale,
That humbly seeks the lowly vale.
The birds poured forth their sweetest lays
In matin songs of grateful praise.
All nature beamed with gladness bright,
And Jordan's wavelets danced in light.
This glorious morn, a favored few
To Olive's mount in sadness drew,
And stood around with listening ear,
Their Saviour's parting words to hear.
With voice divine, and lifted hand,
He gave to them this last command:
"Behold, all power to me is given,
I reign supreme in earth and heaven.
Then go ye forth through all the earth,
And wide proclaim a Saviour's birth;
Tell how he left a throne of light,
And all his robes of kingly might,
And down to earth incarnate came,

Enduring here a life of shame.
Go, point the world to yonder mount,
Where first was opened a cleansing fount;
And bid the nations wash therein,
And thus be pure from every sin.
And I the Holy Ghost will send,
To be your guide till time shall end.
Abide within the city wall
Till this high power from heaven shall fall.
Be not by Satan's power beguiled,
And fear ye not, though oft reviled.
Fight bravely on till life is o'er;
And I am with you evermore."

He ceased; and now a radiance bright
Played all around that form of light;
Sweet music breathed through all the air,
When bands of white-robed seraphs fair
Swift down to earth all shining came,
High heaven's eternal King to claim.

Victorious now the Saviour rose
In glorious triumph o'er his foes;
And mid those bright angelic choirs,
Who struck with joy their golden lyres,
He higher winged his upward way,
Far on to realms of heavenly day.
They gazed till from their mortal sight
His form was veiled in clouds of light;
Then, shouting forth with one accord,
They hail him King, Messiah, Lord!
"O earth!" they cry, "your anthems raise,
Break forth in songs of lofty praise!
Ye hills that gird the city round,
Arise and leap with joyful bound!
Floods clap your hands, and vales rejoice,
Bid all your flowerets raise their voice!
Let Jordan's waves with music flow,
And every stream with rapture glow!
Ye winds of heaven waft the song,
And all ye hills the strains prolong!

Let peal on peal from earth arise,
To meet the anthems of the skies!"
And now around Messiah's feet
Angelic choirs the song repeat.
"All worthy is the Lamb!" they cry;
"And honor, power, and glory high
Shall be to him for ever given,
The sovereign Lord of earth and heaven!"
Ye listening spheres take up the song,
And hallelujahs pour along!
And seraphs strike your harps again,
For earth now shouts a loud AMEN!